FIRST GUIDE TO THE UNIVERSE

P9-DGE-051

Contents

Part 1

OUR EARTH

Contents

Written by:
Jane Chisholm

Designed by:
Roger Priddy

Illustrated by:
Martin Newton
Louise Nevett
Joseph McEwan
Guy Smith

Consultant editor:
Jan Williamson

What is the Earth like?

The Earth is a huge ball of rock spinning round in space. It is one of nine planets which travel round a star called the Sun. Together they are known as the Solar System. Our Sun is just one of many millions of other stars in the Universe. It has a special force called gravity, which keeps the planets travelling round it, and stops them floating into space.

Earth facts

★ The Earth is not perfectly round. It bulges slightly round the middle and is flat at the ends. These are called the North and South Poles. There is a line round the middle called the Equator.

★ The Earth is divided in half at the Equator. The top half is called the northern hemisphere. The bottom half is called the southern hemisphere.

★ Little more than a quarter of the Earth's surface is land. Most of it is in the northern hemisphere, which you can see here. The land is divided into seven blocks called continents.

Water covers nearly ¾ of the Earth's surface. There are four main oceans, which are all linked together.

Nearly 1/8 of the land on Earth is dry desert. Only certain animals and plants can live there.

The Earth is always spinning like a top. It spins on its axis, which is an imaginary line between the Poles.

The Moon is a ball of rock which travels round the Earth. It is 384,000km (230,400mi) away. This is about 20 times as far as from England to Australia. Other planets have their own moons.

The further you are from the Equator, the colder it is. The coldest places on Earth are the North and South Poles. They are always covered with ice.

The Earth is about 40,000km (nearly 25,000mi) all the way round. In a car, it would take about a month to travel round it, without stopping.

Nearly 1/5 of the land on Earth is mountainous. Few people live on mountains. It is often too steep to build on them, and too cold for many things to grow.

Near the Equator, it is hot all year round. In many places, there are thick, jungly forests. The trees sometimes grow as high as a 20-storey building.

The Earth weighs about 6,000 million, million, million tonnes.

The hottest part of the world is an area on each side of the Equator, called the Tropics.

3

Journey to the centre of the Earth

Imagine you are going on a journey down through the Earth. First you have to travel through the rocky, outer layer called the crust.

The top layer of soil is made of tiny specks of crushed rock and the rotting remains of plants. Beneath the soil is a layer of small stones. Beneath that are layers of rock.

Inside the Earth

Here a piece has been cut out of the Earth, so you can see what it looks like inside. It is about 6,300km (3,900mi) to the centre.

Under the crust is a layer of softer rock, called the mantle. At the top of the mantle the rock is hot and liquid. It is moving around all the time.

The centre of the Earth is called the core. The outer core is made of hot, liquid metals — mostly iron and nickel. The inner core is solid metal.

The temperature in the centre could be as high as 4000°C.

The Earth is covered with a hard crust. It varies from about five to 64km thick. No-one has ever dug below the crust. But scientists know roughly what it is like inside.

Inside the rock you may find an underground stream or river.

Caves are often found in limestone, which is worn away easily by water. Rainwater makes cracks and holes in the ground. These get bigger and eventually make caves and tunnels.

Growing tree roots and the burrowing of small animals and insects help to break up the rocks.

Moles

Badgers

Ant-hill

Diamond Mine

Oil Well

Coal mine

In parts of the Sahara Desert, there are underground streams where you can catch fish.

As you go deeper, you will travel through many different types of rocks. There are useful things buried in the ground. Some rocks are made of metals. Others contain precious stones, such as diamonds.

Stalactites

Stalagmites

These strange shapes take hundreds of years to form. They are made by a chemical called lime, which is left by dripping water.

Oil can also be found buried in the rocks. It is probably made from the crushed remains of tiny sea creatures that lived millions of years ago.

You may reach a mine, such as this coal mine. Coal is made from trees that grew millions of years ago. The forests were flooded and pressed down under layers of mud and sand. Slowly they hardened into coal.

5

Why are there hills and valleys?

Some parts of the Earth are flat. Others are hilly and mountainous. The Earth's surface is always changing. But the changes are usually so slow, you are not likely to notice many in your lifetime. Sometimes hot, liquid rock in the mantle squeezes the crust or pushes against This makes bumps in the surface. Over million of years, the bumps turn into mountains.

Sometimes liquid rock from the mantle bursts through the crust. It cools and hardens, leaving a cone-shaped mountain, called a volcano. When hot rock, called lava, bursts out of the top, the volcano is erupting.

Glaciers are slow moving rivers of ice, which carry rocks, soil and stones with them. About a million years ago, in the Ice Age, there were lots of glaciers. Most of them have melted now. But you can still see the steep-sided, flat-bottomed valleys which they carved out.

Cone-shaped mountains are often extinct volcanoes, which do not erupt any more.

New mountains are often steep and high, with pointed peaks.

Waves fling sand and pebbles against the rocks. This can carve strange shapes along the coastline.

Blow hole

A block mountain is made when there is a crack in the Earth's crust.

Sea stacks

Sometimes, when a road or railway cuts through a mountain, you can see different layers of rock.

Sea arch

Just as mountains are being pushed up from below, the land is being shaped from above too. It is slowly worn away by rivers and glaciers, and by rain, wind, ice and sun. Rain and wind carry sand and grit with them. These are thrown against the rocks and rub them, rather like sandpaper. Some rocks are softer than others and wear away more quickly.

The horizon is the point where the sky appears to meet the land. You can never see further than this, because of the Earth's curved surface.

Most people live in valleys, on low land, called plains, or on flat highland areas, called plateaux.

Sometimes, moving rock in the mantle makes the rocks on the surface split and shake. This is called an earthquake.

Look out for rocks that have been worn away into strange shapes.

Old mountains are lower and smoother, because they have been worn away.

Fold mountains are made when the crust is pushed or squeezed. All mountain ranges (groups of mountains) are made like this.

A gorge is a narrow, steep-sided valley, made when a river cuts through hard rock.

7

Water

Earth is the only planet in our Solar System which has water. The amount of water doesn't change. It is reused over and over again. This process is called the "water cycle". Follow boxes 1 to 4 to see how it works.

3 When it is colder, the moisture turns back to water and rain falls from the clouds.

2 The specks of moisture join together to make clouds.

4 When it rains, water sinks into the ground and collects in underground streams and springs. These join rivers and eventually flow back to the sea.

1 The Sun heats the water on the surface of rivers and seas, and turns it into moisture in the air. This is called evaporation.

A river often starts from a spring on a hillside. The place where it starts is called its source.

At first, a river usually flows straight and fast. Then it becomes slower and wider and swings from side to side, to avoid the harder rock.

When a river flows over hard rock onto a softer one, it wears away the soft rock more quickly. This makes a step in the river, called a waterfall.

Meanders

1   **2**   **3**

Ox-bow lake

The bends in a river are called meanders. Over many years, they gradually get wider and wider. After a flood, a river may break over its banks and flow straight on. The loop it leaves behind is called an ox-bow lake.

Rivers help shape the landscape. They carve out the land and carry rocks and soil to the sea. After hundreds of years, steep-sided valleys and gorges form.

The place where a river joins the sea is called the mouth.

A small river flowing into a bigger one is called a tributary.

Sometimes a river drops a lot of mud and stones at the mouth. If the sea does not wash it away, it builds up into a delta, like this.

Sears-Roebuck Tower

The parts of the hill that jut out into the river are called spurs.

Lakes are made when water fills big dips in the ground.

Some shallow lakes dry up if there is not enough rain.

The highest waterfall in the world is Angel Falls in Venezuela, which is nearly 1km (over half a mile) high. It is over twice as tall as the tallest building in the world, which has 110 storeys.

A geyser is a spring of hot water which shoots up through the ground. It is heated by hot rocks in the crust.

9

What's in the sea?

Seas and oceans cover nearly ¾ of the Earth's surface. They are full of all kinds of different plants and animals. Sea water has lots of useful chemicals and minerals in it, including salt. The chemicals are washed from the soil and brought to the sea by rivers. The sea is never still. The water is always moving.

Tsunami are giant waves made by earthquakes

Flying fish

Jellyfish

Sea snake

Most animals and plants live near the surface. The water is warmer there because it is heated by the Sun. The bottom of the sea is very cold and dark.

If you put a message in a bottle and throw it out to sea, it may end up in another part of the world. This is because there are rivers of water in the oceans, called currents. They move in huge circles between hot and cold regions. Currents are caused by the wind and by the Earth's spin.

Corals are small, jelly-like animals, which live in warm, shallow seas. Each coral makes a case of limestone round its body for protection. The case is left behind when it dies. New corals grow on top. Gradually a wall is built up, called a coral reef.

The bottom of the sea is not flat. It is full of mountains and valleys, just like the land. Sea mountains that stick up above the surface are called islands.

Seas can be hot or cold. The hottest sea is the Persian Gulf. It is sometimes as hot as 35°C. The coldest sea, the Arctic Ocean, is frozen in many places.

Sometimes the reef sticks up above the sea to form an island. A circle of coral islands is called an atoll.

Waves

Waves are made by the wind. They look as though they are moving along the surface, but really the water is just going round in circles. If you throw something in the sea, it will go up and down, like this.

Mauna Kea mountain in Hawaii measures 10km (6mi) from the bottom of the sea to its peak. This is higher than the world's highest "land" mountain, Mount Everest.

Fish can breathe under water because they have gills which strain the oxygen from the water.

Seahorse

Shark

The saltiest sea in the world is the Dead Sea. It has so much salt that nothing lives in it. You can float in it easily, without swimming.

Seaweed and small shellfish live near the shore.

Octopus

High tide

Low tide

The deepest part of the sea is Challenger Deep in the Pacific Ocean. It is over 11km (over 7mi) deep. If you dropped a steel ball into it, it would take over an hour to reach the bottom.

On most seashores, the height of the water rises and falls twice a day. These are called high and low tides. Tides are caused by the gravity, or pull, of the Moon and the Sun. This makes two bulges in the oceans on opposite sides of the Earth. As the Earth spins, the bulges move round, producing the different tides.

What's in the sky?

The Earth is wrapped in a layer of air, called the atmosphere. It contains several different gases. One of them is oxygen, which we need in order to live. Another is carbon dioxide, which plants need. The air protects us from dangerous rays from the Sun, called ultra-violet rays. It also acts as a blanket, stopping the Sun's heat from escaping at night. Air is kept in place by the Earth's gravity.

You cannot see air – only the tiny bits of dust floating in it. You can only feel it when it is blowing against you. Wind is moving air.

Air is heavy, but our bodies are made so that we cannot feel it. It gets lighter, the higher you go. By the sea, the air pressing down on your thumbnail weighs about a kilo.

*These layers are not to scale.

The atmosphere is divided into four main layers. It gets thinner gradually and disappears at about 9,500km (6,000mi) from Earth.

1046 km
In the ionosphere, the air is very thin and hot and full of electricity. It gets hotter the higher you go.

Space rocket

Noctilucent clouds are the highest known clouds. They appear after sunset and are probably made of meteor dust.

Meteors are specks of dust from space. Sometimes they fall into the Earth's atmosphere and burn up.

64 km
The next layer is the stratosphere. Most planes fly at this level because the air is calmer.

10 km
The first layer is called the troposphere. It is the narrowest layer*, but contains 90% of the air. Most of our weather happens here. The air gets colder as you go higher.

Clouds are made of tiny drops of water or ice. You find different types of clouds at different heights.

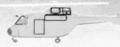

What makes the stars twinkle?

Stars appear to twinkle because light bends as it passes through air. The angle changes with the density and temperature of the air. The light passes through both warm and cold and thick and thin air, so it shines from different directions at once. This looks like twinkling.

What makes the sky change colour?

The Sun's rays contain all the colours of the rainbow. But you cannot see them all. The colour of the sky depends on the position of the Sun. When it is overhead, the sky looks blue. When it is low, the sky may look red, orange or violet.

The outer layer of atmosphere is called the exosphere. It merges with space where there is no air at all.

Weather satellite

In relation to the size of the Earth, the air is as thin as an apple skin.

These are streams of glowing lights, called auroras. You can sometimes see them from countries near the Poles.

Jet streams are high speed winds, which usually blow from the west. Pilots flying east use them to speed up their flight.

Radio waves bounce off the ionosphere and are reflected back to different parts of the Earth.

Some birds can fly as high as about 8km (about 5mi).

On high mountains the air is very thin. Climbers take extra supplies of oxygen with them.

Days and nights

The Sun is about 1,300,000 times as big as Earth. It does not look it, because it is so far away.

The Sun is about 150 million km (93 million mi) away. It would take over 1000 years to get there on a bike.

The Earth spins round at a speed of about 1600km (1000mi) an hour.

The Sun is a huge ball of burning gases, which gives out heat and light. You cannot always see it because of the Earth's spin. When your part of the Earth is turned away from the Sun, you have night, and when it is turned towards the Sun, you have day.

The Earth takes 24 hours to do a complete spin. For about half of this time, your part of the Earth is on the side facing the Sun. During this time, it looks as though the Sun is moving across the sky. In fact it is the Earth that is moving in front of the Sun.

Time changes

It is not the same time all over the world. When you are having midday, people on the other side of Earth have their midnight. The world is divided up into 24 time zones. When it is 1 o'clock in one zone it is 2 o'clock in the one to the east of it and 12 o'clock in the one to the west. When you travel across time zones you have to adjust your watch. The date changes from one day to the next day at a place called the International Date-line.

West   East

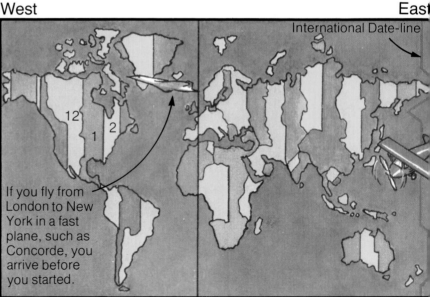

International Date-line

12 1 2

If you fly from London to New York in a fast plane, such as Concorde, you arrive before you started.

If you go right round the world, you cross the International Date-line. Then you lose or gain a whole day.

Shadows

Morning

The Shadows point in the opposite direction to the Sun.

Evening

Midday

The Sun's light travels in straight lines. It cannot go round things. So there are dark shadows behind anything which stands in its way. In the early mornings and evenings, the sun is low and makes long shadows. At midday, the sun is overhead and the shadows are very short. You can use the shadows on a sun dial to help tell the time.

Night

At night you may see the Moon and the stars. Stars are suns too, though they are so far away they look smaller than our Sun. During the day we cannot see them, because our Sun's light is so much stronger than theirs.

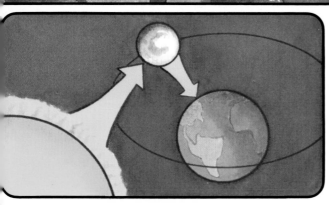

The Moon is a ball of rock which goes round, or orbits, the Earth. It takes about a month to go round. The Moon has no light of its own. You can only see it because the Sun shines on it and it reflects sunlight down to the Earth.

The Moon does not really change shape. It just looks as if it does. At each stage in its orbit round the Earth, a different part of it is lit up. This is how much you would see, if it were in the position shown in the previous picture.

15

The seasons

The Earth spins on its axis and travels round the Sun at the same time. It takes 365¼ days to make a complete trip. We make a year 365 days long. Every four years, we add an extra day to February, to make up for it.

The Earth does not stand upright on its axis. It is always leaning over to one side, so that part of the Earth is tilted towards the Sun. This part gets the most direct heat and light. As the Earth moves round the Sun, the part that is tilted towards it changes. This gives us the seasons.

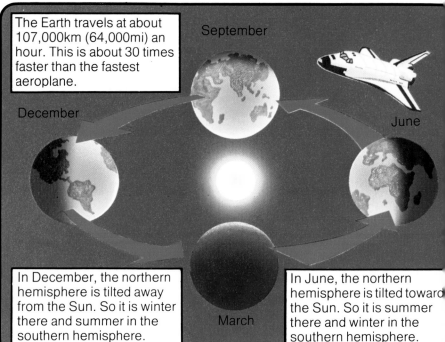

The Earth travels at about 107,000km (64,000mi) an hour. This is about 30 times faster than the fastest aeroplane.

September

December

June

In December, the northern hemisphere is tilted away from the Sun. So it is winter there and summer in the southern hemisphere.

March

In June, the northern hemisphere is tilted toward the Sun. So it is summer there and winter in the southern hemisphere.

Hot and cold places

As the Earth is a ball its surface is curved. When the Sun's rays reach the curved surface of the Earth they get spread out. They have to spread over more surface at the Poles than they do at the Equator. This is why it is always cold at the Poles and always hot at the Equator.

Summers are hotter than winters because when the Earth is tilted towards the Sun the rays are less spread out.

The Sun's rays are always spread out at the Poles, so it is always cold there.

In this picture it is summer in the northern hemisphere.

The Equator is never tilted away from the Sun. That is why it is always hot there, and there are no seasons.

It is winter in the southern hemisphere. The seasons are always the opposite of those in the northern hemisphere.

Why are days different lengths?

In summer, it is not only hotter, but there is more daylight. This is because the part of the Earth that is tilted towards the Sun stays in the Sun's light for longer. The closer you get to the Poles, the greater the difference in daylight between summer and winter.

This diagram shows summer in the southern hemisphere. The red lines stand for daytime. The white lines stand for night. The dotted lines show the part of the Earth you cannot see.

In the far north of countries such as Norway, there is darkness for almost 24 hours in winter.

In summer, there is daylight for almost 24 hours.

At the Equator, days and nights are always 12 hours long.

Eclipses

Sometimes the Moon seems to pass right in front of the Sun. As the Moon and the Sun look the same size in the sky, the Moon covers up the Sun. It gets dark for a short time in a few places on Earth.

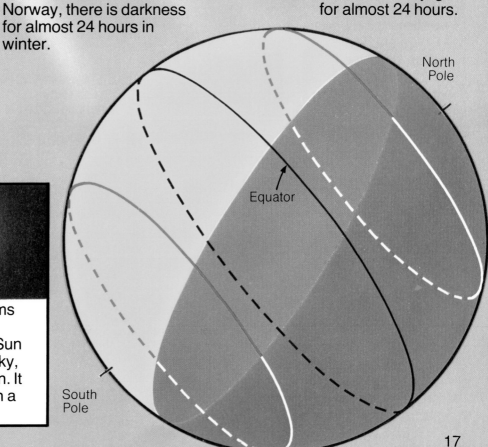

North Pole

Equator

South Pole

Weather

Weather is a combination of air, sun and water. When the air moves, it makes the wind. The Sun gives us warmth. Water makes the clouds, rain and snow.

What makes the wind blow?

Warm air rises, because it is lighter than cold air. As it does so, cold air moves in to take its place. Air is always moving between hot and cold regions. This makes the winds. They do not blow straight between the Poles and the Equator, because the Earth's spin makes them change direction slightly.

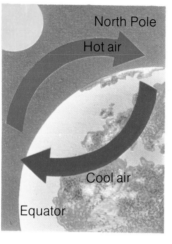

North Pole

Hot air

Cool air

Equator

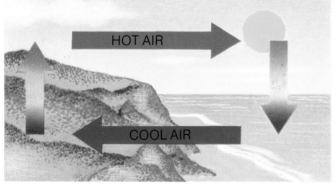

HOT AIR

COOL AIR

Land heats up and cools down faster than the sea, so they are always different temperatures. During the day, cold winds blow in from the sea. At night, warm winds blow out to sea from the land.

Clouds

Warm air can carry more moisture than cold air. When it rises, it gets cooler. Some of the moisture turns to water droplets, or ice crystals (if it is very cold). These join together as clouds. Look at the shapes of clouds. Sometimes they can tell you what kind of weather to expect.

Cirrus are high, wispy clouds, made of ice crystals. Warmer weather coming.

Cirrocumulus are like ripples. Rain soon.

Altocumulus are small and puffy. Water in the clouds sometimes bends the light to make a rainbow ring round the Sun. This is called a corona.

Cirrostratus. You may get a "halo" round the Sun or Moon, because the light is reflected by ice crystals in the clouds.

Flat cumulus clouds Warm, sunny day.

Cumulonimbus is a huge thundercloud.

Nimbostratus is a grey Rain and drizzle soon.

Stratus makes a thick blanket near the ground. When it is very low, it is called fog.

What makes the rain?

As it gets colder, more and more moisture in the air is turned into water droplets. These water droplets bump into each other in the clouds and form bigger drops.

Finally, the water drops become so heavy, the cloud cannot hold them. Then they fall as rain.

The more drops of water in the cloud, the darker it becomes.

It often rains in mountains. Clouds have to rise to get over them. As they rise, they get colder and rain falls.

When the Sun shines through the rain, you may see a rainbow. Sunlight is made of many colours. Normally you do not see them all. The raindrops bend the light, so that you see each colour separately.

They are always in the same order – red, orange, yellow, green, blue, indigo and violet.

When you see a rainbow, it looks like an arch. From high in the sky, you would see it as a complete circle.

Cold Weather

When it is freezing, the water in the clouds turns to specks of ice. The specks get bigger and turn into crystals, which join together to make snowflakes.

Ice specks

Ice crystals

Snowflakes always have six sides.

Snowflakes

If the temperature at ground level is below freezing, the snow melts and falls as rain or sleet.

Frost

At night, the air cools. Some of the moisture in it turns to dew on the ground. If it is very cold, the dew turns to frost.

Storms

Lightning

Thunder

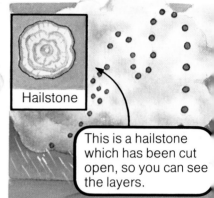

Hailstone

This is a hailstone which has been cut open, so you can see the layers.

In a storm, strong winds make the water droplets in clouds rub against each other. This produces a spark of electricity, called lightning, which shoots out of the cloud. Lightning heats the air around it. The hot air pushes against the cooler air. This makes a loud noise, called thunder. Thunder and lightning happen at the same time. You see the lightning first, because light travels faster than sound.

Hailstones are frozen raindrops. The wind blows them up and down through layers of freezing air, before they fall. Each time, the hailstone gets covered with another layer of ice.

Winds are measured in forces. The strongest, force 12, is a hurricane. They can do a lot of damage. Hurricanes happen in warm, sea areas, where the air is very hot and damp. In some parts of the world, they are called typhoons or cyclones.

A tornado is a fast-moving funnel of twisting air. As it moves, it sucks up everything in its path. Tornadoes happen in very hot, flat places. The wind inside a tornado can move at over 600km (400mi) an hour. A waterspout is a tornado over the sea.

What is your climate like?

The climate is the weather that is usual for your part of the Earth. It depends mainly on your latitude – which means how far you are from the Equator. But other things affect the climate too, such as winds, currents, the height of the land and the distance from the sea.

There are warm and cold currents in the oceans. A warm current called the Gulf Stream warms the coasts of North West Europe.

The climate of the North Atlantic coast is colder, even though it is at the same latitude. This is because of a cold current, the Labrador Current.

In the middle of continents, the climate is often extreme. The summers are very hot and the winters are very cold. At Verkhoyansk in Siberia, the temperature can vary from −70°C to 36°C.

Mountainous regions tend to have more rain.

Inland areas tend to be dry. This is because the wet winds from the sea have lost most of their moisture by the time they reach them.

The sea makes the climate milder. If you live near the coast, or on an island, you probably have cooler summers and warmer winters than inland.

The higher you are above sea level, the colder it is. Mount Kilimanjaro has snow on its peaks all year round, even though it is on the Equator.

The Story of the Earth

The Earth is about 4,600 million years old. It looked very different when it first began. The shape of the land and the climate slowly changed. Certain types of plants and animals appeared. Others died out because they were not so well suited to the conditions. This process is called evolution. Follow this path to see what happened.

The Earth probably began as a huge swirling cloud of dust and gases. Gradually it grew hotter and hotter and turned into a ball of liquid rock.

4,600 million years ago

Then the surface began to cool into a hard crust. Hot, liquid rock burst through the crust in many places. When this cooled, it hardened too.

225 million years ago

All the land on Earth was joined together in one continent, called Pangaea.

The age of dinosaurs – monster reptiles.

280 million years ago

Dimetrodon

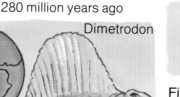

First insects and reptiles

Earth became dryer and covered with deserts. Reptiles took over from amphibians. They have thick, scaly skins, which help them stand the heat and survive better on land.

More amphibians

The Earth was covered with warm, steamy swamps. Later these were buried under layers of sand. After million of years the plants turned into coal.

193 million years ago

Pangaea started splitting apart.

Pterodactyl

Archaeopteryx – the first bird

136 million years ago

The first flowers

The first mammals – animals with fur, that feed their young with milk.

65 million years ago

Horse

Dinosaurs died ou Mammals, trees a plants increased.

800 million years ago

s the Earth cooled, it gave off ouds of steam and gases. The oisture in the clouds cooled into ater drops and heavy rain oured down. This flooded the arth and made the first seas.

2,500 million years ago

Mountains began forming

570 million years ago

As the plants grew, they made oxygen. This made it possible for animals to grow. The first animals were very small and lived in the sea.

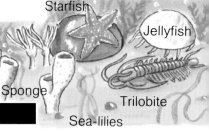

Starfish

Jellyfish

Ammonite

Sponge

Trilobite

Sea-lilies

The first living things grew in the sea. They were neither plants nor animals and were very tiny. Then plants developed.

00 million years ago

400 million years ago

Fish developed. They were the first animals with backbones.

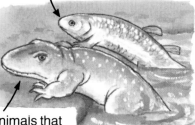

The first amphibians – animals that can live on land and in the sea.

500 million years ago

Sea urchins

Brachiopod

Coral

Ferns grew in swamps. There were still no plants or animals on the dry land.

0 million years ago

e-tooth tiger

Ape

Deer

2 million years ago

Mammoth

The Ice Age. The climate got much colder. Furry animals developed, which could survive well in the cold.

1 million years ago

The early ancestors of people appeared. They lived in caves and made tools from stone. They knew how to use fire, to cook and keep warm.

5,000 million years in the future

Scientists think that in about 5,000 million years, the Earth will end. The Sun will increase its size about 100 times and the Earth will be swallowed up.

Earth words

Here are some of the special Earth words which have been used in the book

Crust, Mantle and Core

The thin, rocky surface of the Earth is called the crust. The layer of softer rock beneath it is the mantle. Some of this rock is hot and liquid and moves around. This causes mountains, volcanoes and earthquakes. The centre of the Earth is called the core.

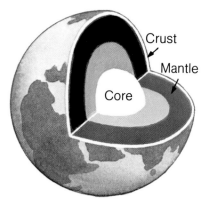

Volcano

A volcano is a mountain or hill with a hole which goes right through the Earth's crust. Sometimes the volcano erupts and lava, steam and gases pour out of the hole. Some volcanoes get blocked up and become extinct. This means they do not erupt anymore.

24

Gravity

Gravity is a special magnetic force which attracts things. The Sun's gravity keeps the planets in orbit. Earth's gravity keeps the Moon spinning round it and stops us from floating around.

Latitude and Longitude

Lines of latitude and longitude are lines invented by scientists to divide up the Earth. Lines of latitude are rings round the Earth, such as the Equator, which goes round the middle. Lines of longitude run between the North and South Poles.

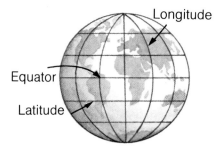

Tides

The tides are the rise and fall of the height of the sea. They are caused by the gravity of the Sun and Moon pulling against the Earth. The highest tides happen when the Sun and Moon are pulling in the same direction.

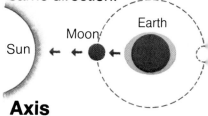

Axis

The axis is the line which the Earth spins round. It runs between the North and South Poles. There isn't really a line there.

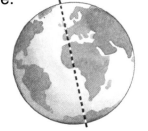

Atmosphere

Atmosphere is the thin blanket of gases which surrounds a planet. Earth's atmosphere contains the gases which people, animals and plants need to live. No other planet in our Solar System has the right atmosphere for us to live on.

Part 2

ROCKETS AND SPACEFLIGHT

Contents

Written by:

Lynn Myring

Designed by:

Roger Priddy
Iain Ashman
Kim Blundell

Illustrated by:

Martin Newton
Louise Nevett
Philip Schramm

Consultant editors:

Carole Turpie
Ian Ridpath

About spaceflight

You live on the planet called Earth. This picture shows where the Earth is in space.

Earth is one of the nine planets which go round and round the Sun.

The Sun and the nine planets together are called the Solar System.

Our Sun is a star. It is the only one in the Solar System. All of the other stars are much further away in space.

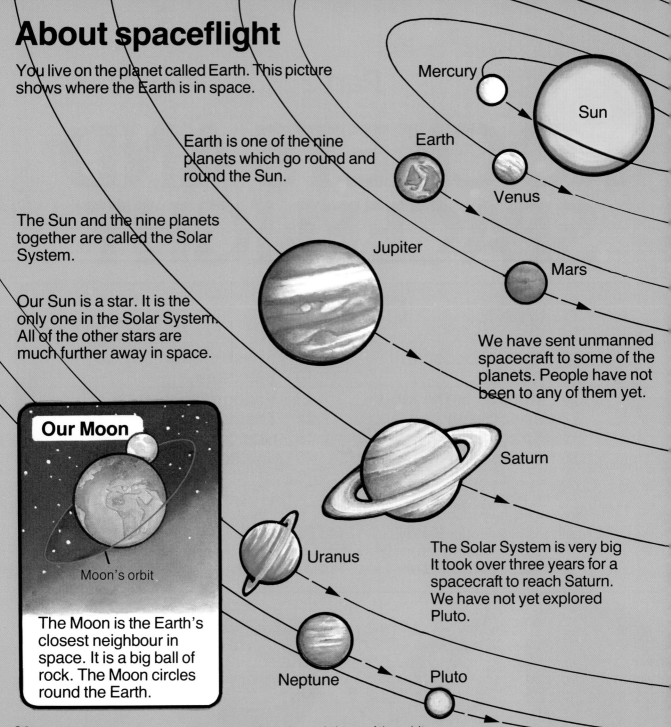

Mercury

Sun

Earth

Venus

Jupiter

Mars

We have sent unmanned spacecraft to some of the planets. People have not been to any of them yet.

Saturn

Our Moon

Moon's orbit

The Moon is the Earth's closest neighbour in space. It is a big ball of rock. The Moon circles round the Earth.

Uranus

The Solar System is very big It took over three years for a spacecraft to reach Saturn. We have not yet explored Pluto.

Neptune

Pluto

This picture is not to scale. It does not show the real shape of the orbits.

Leaving the Earth

Gravity pulls like a big magnet.

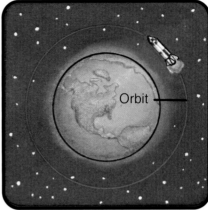

Orbit

Getting off the Earth is the hardest part of a space journey. A strong force called gravity tries to pull the spacecraft back down.

Gravity is what makes things fall to the ground. It is gravity which keeps things on the Earth and stops them flying out to space.

Gravity even affects spacecraft close to the Earth. It makes them circle round and round the Earth. This is called orbiting.

Planning space journeys

Sending a spacecraft to the Moon or a planet is hard because the Earth, Moon and planets are moving all the time. A space journey has to be very carefully planned. It is controlled by lots of people and computers.

A space journey takes so long that a planet will have moved before the spacecraft gets to it. The spacecraft has to be aimed at the place where the planet will be at the end of its journey.

Rockets

A rocket is a very strong kind of engine. It is the only kind powerful enough to fight gravity and launch a spacecraft into space.

The picture below shows a spacecraft and its big launching rockets.

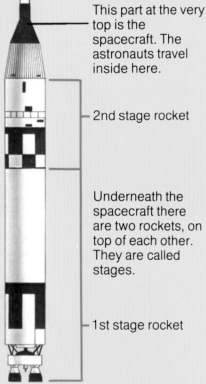

This part at the very top is the spacecraft. The astronauts travel inside here.

2nd stage rocket

Underneath the spacecraft there are two rockets, on top of each other. They are called stages.

1st stage rocket

The stages work one at a time. They fall off when they have used up all their fuel. This makes the load lighter for the next rocket to carry.

How rockets work

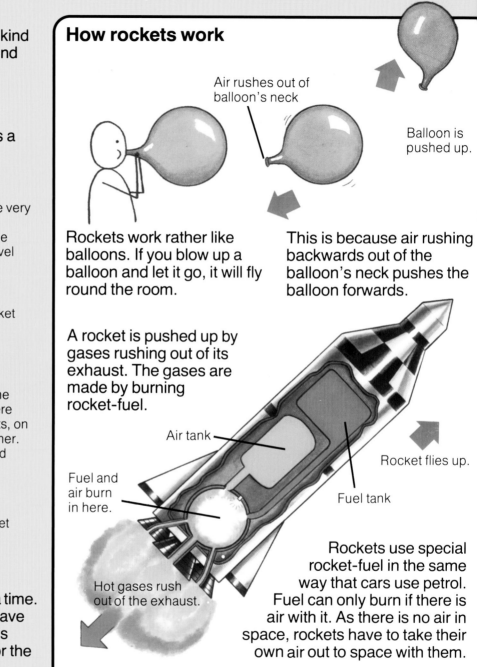

Air rushes out of balloon's neck

Balloon is pushed up.

Rockets work rather like balloons. If you blow up a balloon and let it go, it will fly round the room.

This is because air rushing backwards out of the balloon's neck pushes the balloon forwards.

A rocket is pushed up by gases rushing out of its exhaust. The gases are made by burning rocket-fuel.

Air tank

Rocket flies up.

Fuel and air burn in here.

Fuel tank

Hot gases rush out of the exhaust.

Rockets use special rocket-fuel in the same way that cars use petrol. Fuel can only burn if there is air with it. As there is no air in space, rockets have to take their own air out to space with them.

Rocketing into space

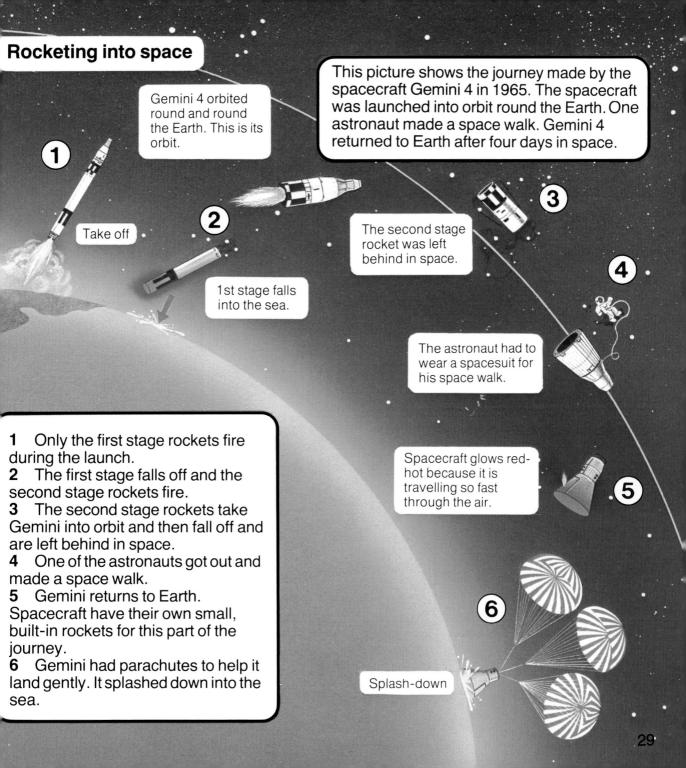

Gemini 4 orbited round and round the Earth. This is its orbit.

This picture shows the journey made by the spacecraft Gemini 4 in 1965. The spacecraft was launched into orbit round the Earth. One astronaut made a space walk. Gemini 4 returned to Earth after four days in space.

1

Take off

2

1st stage falls into the sea.

The second stage rocket was left behind in space.

3

4

The astronaut had to wear a spacesuit for his space walk.

Spacecraft glows red-hot because it is travelling so fast through the air.

5

1 Only the first stage rockets fire during the launch.
2 The first stage falls off and the second stage rockets fire.
3 The second stage rockets take Gemini into orbit and then fall off and are left behind in space.
4 One of the astronauts got out and made a space walk.
5 Gemini returns to Earth. Spacecraft have their own small, built-in rockets for this part of the journey.
6 Gemini had parachutes to help it land gently. It splashed down into the sea.

6

Splash-down

29

Mission to the Moon

One of the most exciting space missions was the first manned landing on the Moon. It took place in 1969. This gigantic, three stage rocket took the three astronauts in the Apollo spacecraft to the Moon. Since then, five other manned Apollo spacecraft have landed on the Moon.

1st stage rocket

2nd stage rocke

USA

The Lunar Module

The astronauts travelled in the Apollo Command Module. This orbited round the Moon, but did not land on it. A special, small spacecraft, called the Lunar Module, landed the astronauts on the Moon. The Lunar Module was stored behind the Apollo Command Module.

3

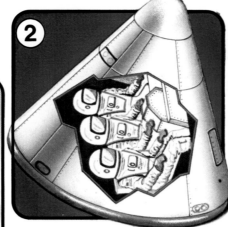

2

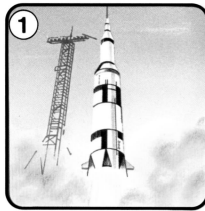

1

The trip to the Moon took about three days. On the way the astronauts took the Luna Module out of storage. The third stage of the Saturn rocket and the Lunar Module storage compartment are lef behind in space.

This picture shows the three astronauts inside the tiny Apollo Command Module. It is the only part which returned to Earth.

The Apollo spacecraft was launched by a huge three stage rocket, called a Saturn 5.

3rd stage rocket — Apollo spacecraft —

The Lunar Module is stored inside here.

Apollo Command Module

This launch escape rocket takes the Command Module to safety if there is an accident at take-off.

6

5

4

Two of the astronauts got into the Lunar Module and flew it to the Moon. Here it is landing. It has its own small, built-in rockets.

After exploring on the Moon the astronauts returned to the Command Module. It had stayed in orbit above the Moon with one astronaut on board.

The bottom part of the Lunar Module was left behind on the Moon. Only the top part took off and flew back to the Apollo Command Module.

The Lunar Module was left behind in space. The three astronauts flew home in the Command Module. It had small rockets of its own too.

On the Moon

The fourth Apollo Moon mission took a moon-buggy, so that the astronauts could explore further.

The astronauts had to wear spacesuits when they were on the Moon. Look on the next page to find out about spacesuits.

Lunar Module

Astronaut

Moon buggy

31

Spacesuits

Astronauts do not have to wear special spacesuits when they are on board their spacecraft. They have to put them on if they go outside into space or on the Moon or another planet. There is no air to breathe in space. It i[s] hotter than an oven in the Sun's light, but colder than a freezer in the shade. This pictur[e] shows two astronauts in space.

Astronauts sometimes have to leave their spacecraft to do repairs or set up experiments.

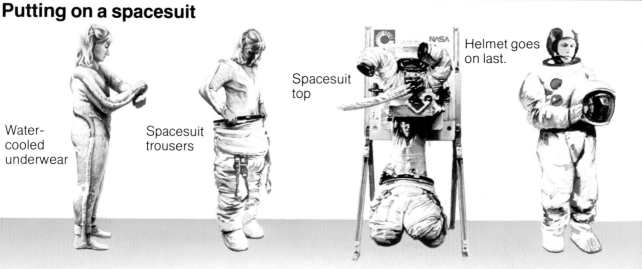

They wear spacesui[ts] and are connected t[o] their spacecraft b[y] long cable[s.]

The spacesuit has ai[r] tanks. It also keeps th[e] astronaut at the righ[t] temperature[.]

Putting on a spacesuit

Water-cooled underwear

Spacesuit trousers

Spacesuit top

Helmet goes on last.

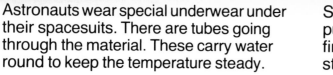

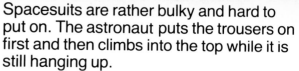

Astronauts wear special underwear under their spacesuits. There are tubes going through the material. These carry water round to keep the temperature steady.

Spacesuits are rather bulky and hard to put on. The astronaut puts the trousers on first and then climbs into the top while it is still hanging up.

This is the spacesuit worn by the Shuttle astronauts. Look on the next page to find out about the Shuttle.

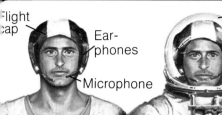

Flight cap

Ear-phones

Microphone

Bubble helmet

Outer helmet

Gold layer

This outer helmet goes on top of the bubble helmet. The front is covered with a thin layer of real gold which acts like sunglasses.

Astronauts wearing spacesuits talk to each other by radio. Their caps have a microphone and earphones. A clear bubble helmet goes over the head and joins up to the suit. It fills with air for the astronaut to breathe.

Astronauts can even go to the toilet as the spacesuit has a kind of nappy inside.

Floating in space like this is a very strange feeling. Astronauts have said that it feels a bit like swimming in deep, still water.

Glove

Shoes

Cable

The airtanks and radio are inside this big backpack. It is fixed to the suit top. It has enough air for seven hours.

Backpack

The backpack also pumps the water round the underwear.

The suit has a tiny computer which makes sure that everything is working. It tells the astronaut if anything breaks down and shows how to mend the fault.

Spacesuits are made from very tough materials, so they do not tear easily.

This cable keeps the astronaut attached to the spacecraft. It is covered in thin gold.

33

Space Shuttle

The Shuttle is the newest kind of spacecraft. It is the first one which can be used more than once. It will fly out to space and back to Earth many times.

These are the Shuttle's three main engines. It has other smaller ones.

The Shuttle is the first spacecraft to have wings. They help it to glide back to Earth.

These doors open when the Shuttle is out in space. This helps to keep the spacecraft cool and exposes the special equipment inside.

Rocket exhaust

United States

The storage area inside here.

Wing

Flying the Shuttle

1

The Shuttle has its own rockets but needs two big booster rockets and an extra fuel tank to launch it into space.

2

The booster rockets and fuel tank fall off when they run out of fuel. The boosters can be used more than once too.

3

The Shuttle has a large storage area for taking things up into space. It can open up when the Shuttle is in orbit.

This picture shows parts of the Shuttle cut away, so that you can see inside.

The living-quarters and flight-deck are inside the small nose part of the Shuttle.

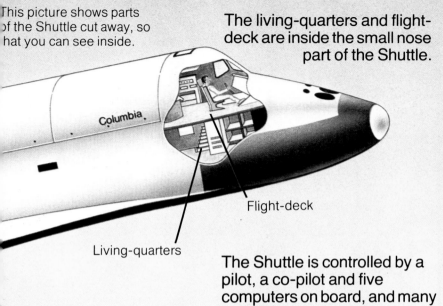

Columbia

Flight-deck

Living-quarters

Special tiles on the outside help to keep the Shuttle cool.

The Shuttle is controlled by a pilot, a co-pilot and five computers on board, and many people at mission-control on Earth.

4 The Shuttle returns to Earth like a glider. It falls though the air glowing red-hot because it is going at high speed.

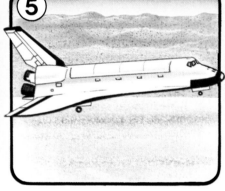

5 It lands like an ordinary plane, on a very long runway. The Shuttle takes only one hour to come to Earth from space.

Shuttle missions

The Shuttle will be used to put new satellites into orbit and bring old or broken ones to Earth.

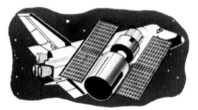

The Shuttle took the Hubble Space Telescope into orbit around the Earth. It is used to study the stars and is controlled from Earth.

The Shuttle is also booked to take scientists and a laboratory out to orbit and back again. They will do lots of experiments in space.

On board a spacecraft

One of the strangest things about being in space is that everything becomes completely weightless because there is no gravity. There is no ''up'' or ''down''. Things will just float in mid-air unless they are fixed to something.

Control instruments

The instruments are all one way up. The crew try to stay the same way up too.

Astronauts sleep in sleeping bags fixed to the ''walls''. They cannot lie down as they are weightless.

Astronauts have to hold the special handles when they are doing things, otherwise they push themselves into mid-air.

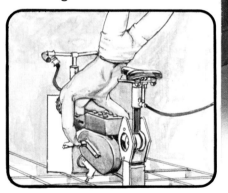

Weightlessness makes the muscles weak. The astronauts use exercise machines to keep fit and healthy.

The spacecraft is controlled most of the time by people at mission control on Earth. The astronauts can take over if necessary.

Space travel makes some astronauts feel sick at first. This may be because they are weightless.

This is a storage area for equipment. Things have to be put away inside cupboards, otherwise they will float around in the spacecraft.

Handles

Astronauts eat ordinary food packed in cans which they heat up in a tray. They have to be careful that the food does not float away.

Food tray

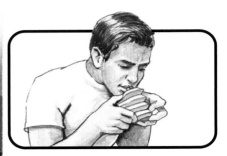

Even liquids float in space. Astronauts have to suck their drinks out of tubes as they cannot use cups.

Baths are a problem. The astronauts shower inside a big bag which stops the water flying about.

The weightless astronauts move by pushing against the walls and using handles. They seem to be flying.

Space station Skylab

A space station is a spacecraft big enough for a crew to live and work in for several weeks. This is the space station Skylab. It was launched into orbit round Earth in 1973.

Space stations stay in orbit a[l] of the time, even when there i[s] no crew on board. Three crews visited Skylab. Each one stayed in space for 56 days.

This is a telescope for studying the Sun.

The Skylab crews did lots of scientific experiments. The most important was to show that people could live in spac[e] for a long time.

Skylab was the biggest spacecraft ever made. Inside it was as large as a three-storey house.

These solar panels powered the telescope

Sunshade

This solar panel powered electrical equipment inside Skylab. There should have been another one on the othe[r] side.

Solar panel

Skylab was damaged when it was launched. One of the solar panels and part of the protective outer skin were torn off.

The first crew had to repair Skylab. They put up a sunshade over the damaged outer skin, to stop Skylab overheating.

The second crew put up this gold foil sunshade.

The astronauts and equipment are inside this part of Skylab.

Going to Skylab

The astronauts got into Skylab through doors here.

Skylab

Apollo spacecraft

Skylab was launched without a crew. The astronauts went up to it and back again in Apollo spacecraft, like the ones which went to the Moon.

The Apollo had to be joined to Skylab. This is called docking. The astronauts crawled into Skylab through special doors in the Apollo and Skylab.

Skylab's end

Skylab was in a low orbit close to Earth. Gravity was able to pull it back to Earth in 1979 after six years in space. The spacecraft broke into

pieces as it fell through the air. Most of the pieces burnt up before reaching Earth. A few fell into the sea and some landed in Australia.

Working on Skylab

The crews did lots of work in Skylab. Here are some of the experiments and studies they did.

One crew studied the comet Kohoutek which passed close to Earth in 1973.

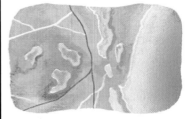

This picture shows a view of Earth from Skylab. The crews took thousands of photographs of the Earth and Sun.

One crew took a spider into space to see if it could spin a web while weightless. The first one was not very good, but later ones were better.

Satellites

There are many small, unmanned spacecraft in orbit close to the Earth. They are called satellites. Satellites carry instruments and do lots of useful jobs. This picture shows a satellite called Landsat. It studies the Earth.

Solar panel

Landsat takes pictures of the Earth and sends them down to special television sets on the ground.

These pictures help us to make maps. They also help us to find new supplies of things like oil and gas.

Landsat's cameras and instruments point down towards Earth.

Weather satellites

Satellites have solar panels to provide power for their instruments. The solar panels make electricity from sunlight.

Other satellites watch the weather. They help scientists to make the weather forecasts.

Television by satellite

1 Several satellites are used to send television pictures from one part of the world to another. The pictures are sent as radio signals.

2 These signals are beamed up through space to the satellite. They bounce off the satellite and back to Earth, but to a different place.

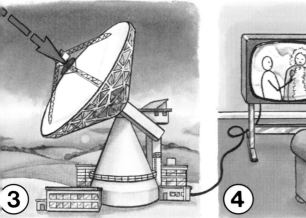

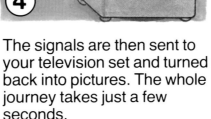

3 The signals are picked up on Earth by big dish-shaped aerials like the one above. The satellite has dish-shaped aerials as well.

4 The signals are then sent to your television set and turned back into pictures. The whole journey takes just a few seconds.

Going round the Earth

The Earth spins round once every day.

Television satellites move in time with the Earth. This means that they stay above the same place all the time.

Satellites which study the Earth orbit much faster. They see the whole world once every few hours.

41

Visiting the planets

People have travelled in space only as far as our Moon. Unmanned spacecraft, called probes, are used to explore the planets, as these are very far away.

This is Voyager 2, a probe that went to Jupiter in 1979 and Saturn in 1981.

Probes are launched into space by rockets.

Aerial for sending radio signals back to Earth

TV cameras

These television cameras took pictures of Saturn. These were then beamed back to Earth as radio signals.

Messages from Mars

This picture shows the Viking lander probe on the planet Mars. It is sending pictures and information to Earth.

Mars

Earth

The information and pictures travel across space as radio signals. They take 20 minutes to reach Earth from Mars.

Here are scientists studying the pictures and information from the probe on Mars. They are using a computer.

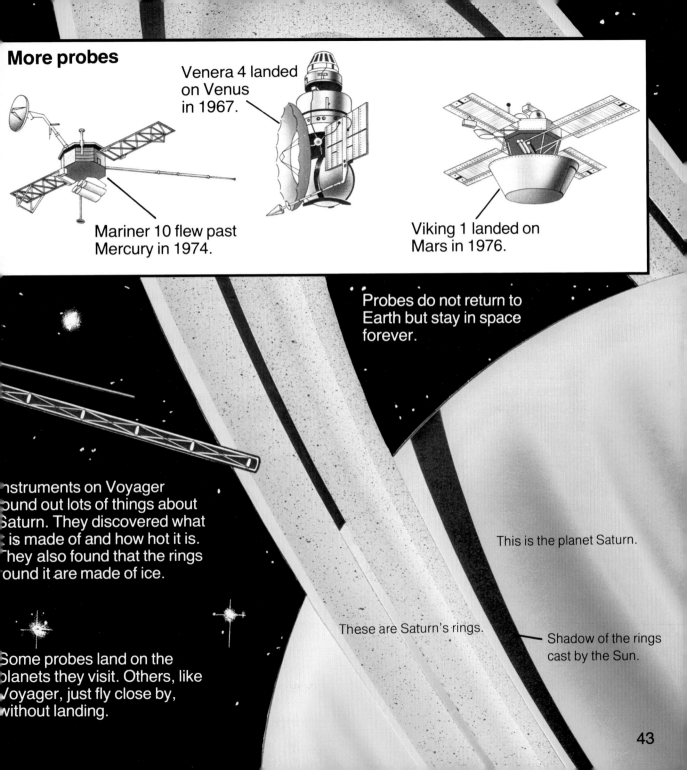

More probes

Venera 4 landed on Venus in 1967.

Mariner 10 flew past Mercury in 1974.

Viking 1 landed on Mars in 1976.

Probes do not return to Earth but stay in space forever.

Instruments on Voyager found out lots of things about Saturn. They discovered what it is made of and how hot it is. They also found that the rings round it are made of ice.

This is the planet Saturn.

These are Saturn's rings.

Shadow of the rings cast by the Sun.

Some probes land on the planets they visit. Others, like Voyager, just fly close by, without landing.

43

The future in space

One day people may live and work in huge space cities like the one pictured here. It is about as big as New York and not at all like a spacecraft. The space city has artificial gravity and is full of air in the parts where people live. There are houses, parks, farms, offices, schools, factories, shops and even sports centres – in fact, everything that people want.

The space city would have solar panels to make electricity from sunlight.

Satellites would be used for sending messages between the Earth and the space city.

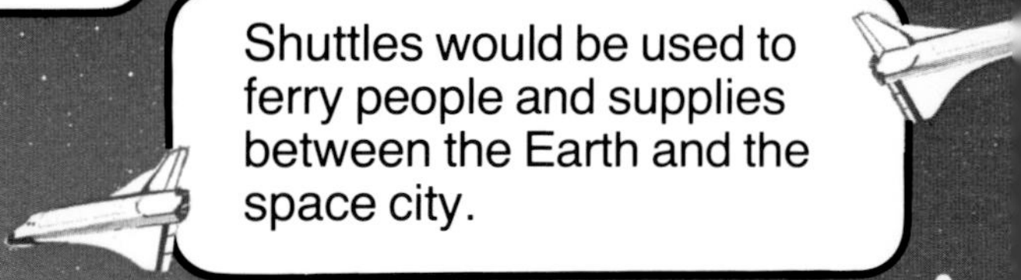

Shuttles would be used to ferry people and supplies between the Earth and the space city.

In the future, we may put large solar panels into space. These would make electricity from sunlight and beam it down to Earth.

Inside a space city

The sky would look slightly different from a space city. You would be able to see Earth and would have a different view of the Moon.

This picture shows what it could be like inside a space city. This is the ring-shaped part where people live. It has gravity, air, plants, buildings and even a river. There are big windows to let in sunlight and heat.

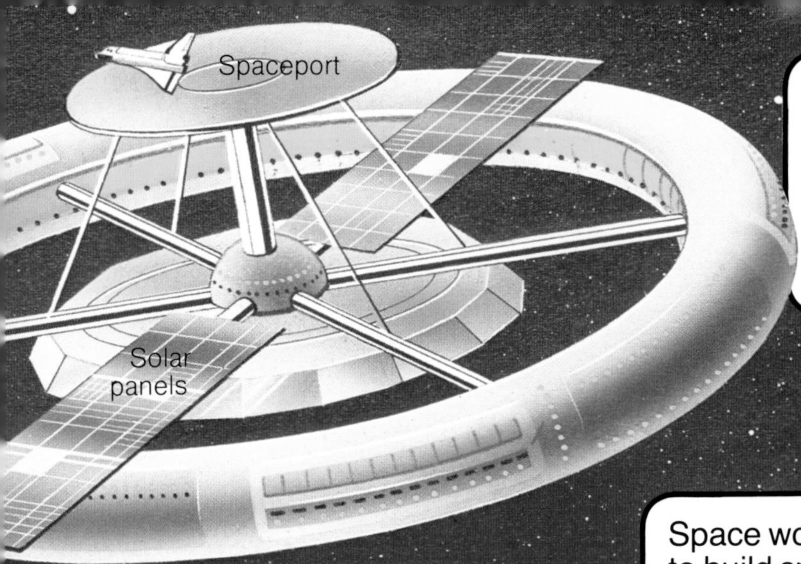

Spaceport

Solar panels

People would live and work inside this ring-shaped tube. The middle part of the space city is an industrial area and spaceport, where there is no gravity.

The space city would be made in space. It could be built from metals and other things mined on the Moon and planets.

Space would be a good place to build spacecraft. There would be no need to build the huge rockets needed to launch them from Earth.

Living on Mars

People would have to wear spacesuits if they went outside the city.

This picture shows what a city on Mars might be like. It is built under domes that are filled with air and kept warm. There is little air on Mars and it gets very cold. A colony on the Moon could be similar to this one.

Star travel fantasy

This picture shows what a spacecraft of the future might be like. It has left our Solar System and is travelling to another star. Scientists think that there could be a planet rather like Earth there.

At the moment star travel seems to be impossible. This is because the stars are so very far away. It would take much longer than a person's lifetime to travel to them in the spacecraft which we have today.

Even the nearest star is too far away to visit. If stone age people had been able to make a spacecraft and set out on a journey to the nearest star, they would be only about half way there by now, 50,000 years later.

Perhaps the crew of a star ship could be frozen or put into a deep sleep for the long journey to the stars. Computers and robots might look after the spacecraft and wake up the crew when they arrived.

Going through a space warp

People who write stories about space and some scientists have thought about the problems of star travel. They have imagined new ways of travelling through space. This picture shows one idea – a space warp.

The space warp is like a hole in space. The star ship goes into the hole in one part of space, but comes out again in a completely different place. The whole journey could take just a few seconds.

Travelling space city

Perhaps people will go to other stars in huge travelling space cities. Many people would be born, have children and die before arriving.

Beaming through space

Another idea is to beam people through space. They would be broken down into tiny specks for the journey and joined together at the other end.

Spaceflight words

Here are some of the special spaceflight words which have been used in this book.

Solar System

The Solar System is made up of our Sun and the nine planets which orbit round it. We have sent unmanned spacecraft to explore some of the Solar System.

Planets

A planet is a big ball of rocks and gases which orbits the Sun. Earth is a planet. People have not been to any other planets.

Moon

Our Moon is a ball of rock which orbits the Earth. There have been six manned missions which landed on the Moon. Some other planets have moons of their own too.

Stars

The stars are gigantic balls of hot burning gases. Our Sun is a star. The other stars are very far away. They are too far to visit by spacecraft.

Spacecraft

A spacecraft is a vehicle which travels in space. Some spacecraft have people on board. Others, such as satellites, are unmanned.

Rockets

Rockets are a very strong kind of engine. They are used to launch and power spacecraft. Rockets are very large.

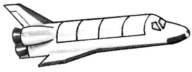

Probes

Probes are unmanned spacecraft which are sent to study other planets. They have special equipment on board, which sends back to Earth lots of pictures and information.

Shuttle

The Shuttle is the first spacecraft which can be used more than once. It made its first spaceflight in 1981.

Solar panels

Solar panels are used to power the equipment on board spacecraft such as probes and satellites. They make electricity out of sunlight.

Part 3
SUN, MOON AND PLANETS

Contents

Written by:
Lynn Myring
Sheila Snowden

Designed by:
Roger Priddy

Illustrated by:
Martin Newton
Louise Nevett
Philip Schramm

Consultant editor:
Carole Turpie

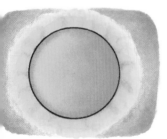

Our part of space

Our part of space is called the Solar System. It is made up of the Sun, nine planets which go round it, 43 moons which go round the planets and a band of space rocks called the Asteroid Belt. The Sun is so big we can show only part of it on this page. It is a huge ball of burning gases. The planets are much smaller balls of rocks and gases or liquids and gases. All of the moons and asteroids are rocky.

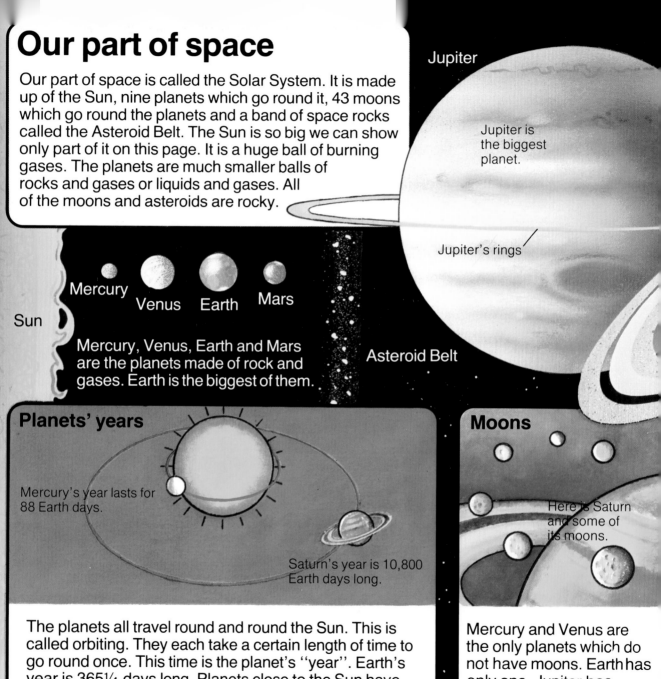

Jupiter

Jupiter is the biggest planet.

Jupiter's rings

Sun

Mercury

Venus

Earth

Mars

Mercury, Venus, Earth and Mars are the planets made of rock and gases. Earth is the biggest of them.

Asteroid Belt

Planets' years

Mercury's year lasts for 88 Earth days.

Saturn's year is 10,800 Earth days long.

The planets all travel round and round the Sun. This is called orbiting. They each take a certain length of time to go round once. This time is the planet's ''year''. Earth's year is 365¼ days long. Planets close to the Sun have shorter years than those further away from the Sun.

Moons

Here is Saturn and some of its moons.

Mercury and Venus are the only planets which do not have moons. Earth has only one. Jupiter has 16 and Saturn has 18.

Saturn

Jupiter, Saturn, Uranus and Neptune are giant planets very much bigger than Earth. They are made of liquids and gases and do not have hard surfaces like Earth's. Pluto is the smallest planet and is made of ice and rock.

— Uranus's rings

Uranus

Plut

Jupiter, Saturn, Neptune*
and Uranus have rings
going round them. You
can find out more about
these later on in this book.

Neptune

Why are there days and nights?

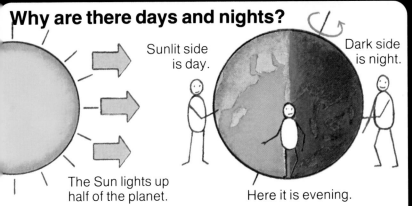

Sunlit side
is day.

Dark side
is night.

The Sun lights up
half of the planet.

Here it is evening.

The planets spin like tops as they orbit round the Sun. Different parts of their surfaces are lit by the Sun as they spin. This gives them day and night. They all spin at different speeds and so have different length days. Earth spins once every 24 hours.

The planets are all a very long way away from the Sun. If the pictures above were made into a scale model of the Solar System, this is how far from the model Sun some planets would have to be.
Mercury – 38m (12.5ft) about the length of a room.
Earth – 98m (321ft) about as long as a football pitch.
Jupiter – 506m (1,660ft) about as long as five football pitches.
Pluto – 3,835m (2.3mi) about 45 minutes walk.

The Sun

The Sun is the most important part of the Solar System. It holds all the planets in their positions in space and gives them their light and heat. Without the Sun, the Solar System would be dark and cold.

This picture shows the Sun as if a slice had been cut out of it so that you can see inside. The Sun is not solid like Earth. It is a huge ball of fiery gases.

The Sun is made of the gases hydrogen and helium. It does not burn like an ordinary fire on Earth. The Sun burns by turning hydrogen into helium.

**WARNING
NEVER LOOK AT THE SUN.**
It is so hot and bright
it can hurt your eyes.

The Sun is the hottest thing in the Solar System. It reaches an incredible 15 million °C in the centre. A pin head as hot as this could kill someone standing 150km (90mi) away.

Our nearest star

This is how our Sun may look from Triton, one of Neptune's moons.

Our Sun is actually a star, like the stars you can see at night. It looks different to us on Earth because we are closer to the Sun than to other stars. From more distant planets, the Sun probably looks like a big bright star in the sky.

The surface of the Sun is much cooler than the inside. It reaches about 6,000°C which is 60 times hotter than boiling water.

Giant jets of gases shoot up from the surface of the Sun. They are called solar flares. The whole surface of the Sun bubbles like boiling soup.

Solar flare

These dark patches are called sunspots. They are areas of gas which are cooler than the rest of the surface. These sunspots are many times bigger than the Earth.

Sunspots

The Sun is much bigger than all the planets put together. It would take over a million Earths to fill a hollow ball the size of our Sun.

If there were no Sun, there would be no life on Earth. Plants and animals need the Sun's heat and light in order to live and grow.

Plants use sunlight to make their food.

Solar flares

Earth's size

This gigantic solar flare was studied by astronauts on the spacecraft Skylab. It is many times bigger than the Earth.

Studying the Sun

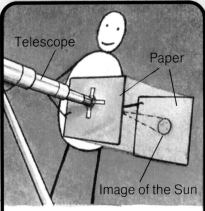

Telescope

Paper

Image of the Sun

It is dangerous to look at the Sun. Astronomers focus a telescope so that it makes a picture of the Sun on a sheet of paper.

The Moon

Moon reflects the Sun's light.

The Moon is the biggest and brightest thing in the sky at night. It shines but it does not make its own light. The Moon just reflects light from the Sun. The Moon is Earth's closest neighbour in space but it is still a long way away. The journey to the Moon is as long as going round the Earth about ten times.

The Moon is much smaller than Earth. It would take 81 Moons to weigh as much as one Earth and 50 Moons to f a hollow ball the size of Earth

The Man in the Moon

The Moon is said to look like a face from Earth. The "face" is made of areas of dark rocks.

Farside of the Moon

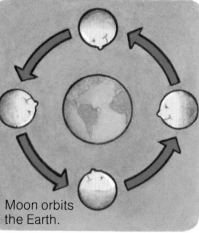

Moon orbits the Earth.

The Moon orbits round the Earth once every 27⅓ days. It always keeps the same half facing the Earth. No-one had

Spacecraft orbiting the Moon.

seen the farside of the Moon until 1959 when the Luna 3 probe orbited the Moon and sent back pictures.

Why does the Moon change shape?

From Earth the Moon seems to change its shape. It grows from a thin sliver into a bigger crescent. Then it becomes a Half-Moon which swells until it is a whole Full-Moon. It slowly shrinks back to a half, to a crescent and down to a sliver. The whole process takes about a month and is shown in the picture below. The different shapes are called phases.

You cannot see all these phases of the Moon at the same time

The Moon is not really changing shape. It just looks as if it is from Earth. This is because we see different parts of the Moon's lit up side as it orbits round the Earth. Look at the pictures below and follow the Moon on its journey round Earth.

New-Moon

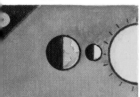

Crescent

Half-Moon

Gibbous Moon

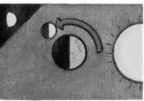

Full-Moon

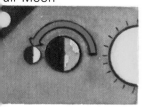

Gibbous Moon

Half-Moon

Crescent

When the Moon is directly between the Earth and the Sun we cannot see any of the lit up side at all. Strangely, this phase is called a New-Moon. The lit up side becomes visible as the Moon moves round. We can see a Half-Moon when it is a quarter of the way round its orbit. When Earth is between the Sun and the Moon we can see all of the lit up side as a Full-Moon. After this, less and less of lit up side is visible from Earth.

On the Moon

Things are very different on the Moon than on the Earth. We know a lot about what it is like on the Moon because astronauts have been there. This picture shows two of them on the Moon.

Earth can be seen in the sky, just as the Moon can be seen from Earth. The Earth seems to change its shape and go through phases from the Moon.

The sky is always black even in the daytime.

Spacecraft and astronaut

The Moon has mountains, flat areas, hilly areas, crevices, craters and dead volcanoes. It is a bare, dead world, where nothing lives or grows.

Moon craters

There are millions of holes called craters on the Moon.

The astronauts had to wear spacesuits and use airtanks on the Moon as there is no air there. They carried out lots of experiments.

Craters vary in size from tiny specks to holes bigger than cities. Some are so big they can be seen from Earth.

This machine measured moonquakes.

The craters were probably made by stray space rocks, called meteorites, which crashed into the Moon, millions of years ago.

The surface of the Moon is bare greyish rock. It is all bumpy and stoney and covered with a layer of fine dust. It is very dry as there is no water at all on the Moon.

Moon days and nights

The Moon has days and nights that are each 14 Earth days long. The Sun shines all the time during the long day and makes the Moon hotter than boiling water. At night the Moon is dark and freezing – much colder than ice.

Moon walk

Everything weighs less on the Moon than on Earth.

Astronauts could jump higher on the Moon than they could on Earth.

Astronauts walking on the Moon moved with big, swaying strides, bouncing up and down as they walked. They moved in this funny way as they weighed much less on the Moon than they did on Earth. On Earth an astronaut in his spacesuit weighed 135kg (300lb) but on the Moon he weighed only 23kg (50lb). This is because the Moon has less gravity than Earth. Gravity is the force which pulls things to the ground.

Moon soil and Moon weather

Things cannot live on the Moon because there is no air or water there. The astronauts brought Moon soil and rocks back to Earth for scientists to study.

They found that with air and water, plants could grow in Moon soil on Earth.

Footprint in Moon dust

There is no wind or rain or any other weather on the Moon. This means the astronauts' footprints will never be blown or washed away.

The Moon is a completely silent place. Noises cannot be heard as there is no air to carry sounds from one place to another.

The planet Mercury

This picture shows Mercury, the closest planet to the Sun. Being close to the Sun makes Mercury very hot during the day. It is very cold at night.

Mercury is a small planet, only slightly bigger than our Moon. Photographs of Mercury were taken by spacecraft which flew very close. These show that it looks like our Moon.

The surface of Mercury is covered in craters and dusty stoney soil. There is no air or water on Mercury. It is a dry, dead, desert of a world.

Mercury's craters are like the Moon's.

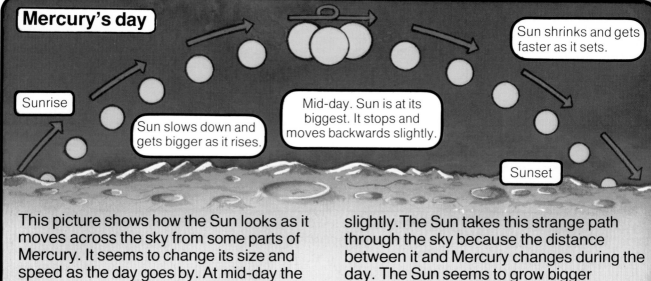

Mercury's day

Sunrise

Sun slows down and gets bigger as it rises.

Mid-day. Sun is at its biggest. It stops and moves backwards slightly.

Sun shrinks and gets faster as it sets.

Sunset

This picture shows how the Sun looks as it moves across the sky from some parts of Mercury. It seems to change its size and speed as the day goes by. At mid-day the Sun even stops and goes backwards slightly. The Sun takes this strange path through the sky because the distance between it and Mercury changes during the day. The Sun seems to grow bigger because Mercury is moving closer to it.

A visit to Venus

Venus is the hottest planet in the Solar System. It reaches a scorching 480°C which is hot enough to make things glow a dull red.

Venus is covered in thick clouds of poisonous sulphuric acid. These clouds never clear to let sunshine through and so it is always dull and dreary.

Why Venus is hot

Heat bounces off the clouds.

The thick clouds make Venus hot as they trap the Sun's heat. It can go through the clouds down to the surface but cannot get out again.

Backward planet

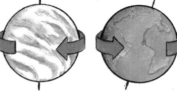

Venus spins in the opposite direction to the other planets. It is very slow and takes 243 Earth days to spin once. This is longer than the time Venus takes to orbit the Sun, which is 225 Earth days. So, a day on Venus is longer than a year.

It would be impossible for people to visit Venus. They would be roasted by the heat, pushed over by the winds, crushed and suffocated by the thick air and poisoned by the acid clouds.

Lightning

Crevice

The air on Venus is made of carbon dioxide gas. It is 60 times thicker than the air on Earth.

The surface of Venus is dry, rocky and very hot. There are deep cracks called crevices and volcanoes.

Boulder

What it is like on Mars

This picture shows what it is like on Mars. Mars is sometimes called the Red Planet because it is made of red rocks. The rocks are coloured by rust. Even the sky is pink on Mars. It is coloured by dust from the rocks.

The surface of Mars is like a rocky desert. There are many boulders and craters, high mountains, deep canyons and dusty sand dunes.

A Martian year is almost two Earth years long. A day on Mars is only half an hour longer than an Earth day.

The air on Mars is very thin and made of carbon dioxide gas. The winds are strong enough to whip up dust storms that cover the whole planet. Mars is about half the size of Earth.

Mars is further from the Sun than Earth is. This makes it cold. The temperature is always below freezing point.

Dust storm

Crater

Rocks

Dunes

Viking spacecraft on Mars

Ice caps

Mars has ice caps at the North and South poles. This is the only water left on Mars. They melt slightly in the summer and shrink in size.

Mars moons

Deimos

Phobos

Mars has two tiny moons, called Deimos and Phobos. Phobos orbits Mars three times a day and goes through most of its phases in each orbit.

Mars has the largest volcano in the Solar System. It is called Olympus Mons. All the volcanoes on Mars are dead and do not erupt anymore.

Volcano ——

| Wispy clouds

Scientists think that there may have been lots of water on Mars millions of years ago. There are dried up river beds and rocks which look as if they were worn down by water.

We know a lot about Mars because spacecraft have landed there and sent pictures back to Earth.

The Asteroid Belt

There are thousands of rocks going round the Sun in the space between Mars and Jupiter. They are called the asteroids.

Most asteroids are pebble-sized but some are as big as skyscrapers and a few even larger than cities.

Asteroids are very knobbly and cratered.

The asteroids may be the shattered remains of a planet which exploded millions of years ago. Or they may be left over rocks which did not form into a planet when the other planets formed.

Jupiter and Saturn, the giant planets

Jupiter and Saturn are quite alike. They do not have rocky surfaces like Earth. They are made of gases and liquids. This picture shows the vast, swirling clouds of gases on Jupiter.

This is Io, one of Jupiter's 16 moons. It is the only place in the Solar System, apart from Earth and Venus, which has live volcanoes.

The clouds of gases rise up and fall like waves. They make bands of different colours as they contain different chemicals.

The cloud layer is about 1,000km (625mi) thick. Below this is liquid hydrogen which does not exist naturally on Earth.

Fierce winds blow all the time, swirling the clouds into bands and whirling storms, which look like spots in the cloud tops.

Huge streaks of lightning flash between the clouds.

Jupiter and Saturn spin faster than any of the other planets, although they are the biggest. They each turn once in about 11 Earth hours.

It is impossible to land on Jupiter as it do not have a rocky surfa

Jupiter and Saturn are a long way from the Sun and so take a long time to orbit it. Jupiter's year is 12 Earth years long, Saturn's is 29½.

Jupiter is the giant of the Solar System. It would take 1,300 Earths to fill a ball the size of Jupiter.

Bulging planets

Jupiter and Saturn are not as round as the rocky planets. They are rather flattened at the top and bottom and bulge out round their middles.

The floating planet

Saturn is made of chemicals which are lighter than water. This means that the planet could float, if there was a sea big enough to put it in.

The Giant Red Spot

Two Earths could fit into Jupiter's Giant Red Spot.

A huge storm has been blowing on Jupiter for many hundreds of years. It is called the Giant Red Spot because of its size and colour.

Saturn's rings

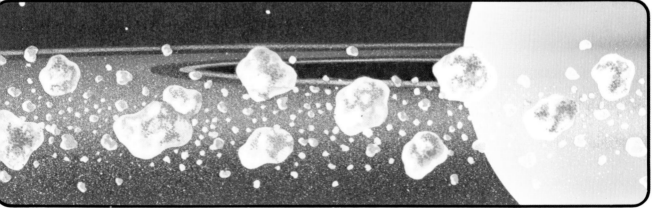

Saturn is circled by a series of rings. They orbit round the middle of the planet. The rings are not solid but made of pieces of rock and ice. Most of the pieces are pebble-sized, though some are like dust and others like boulders. The rings are thin and flat. They stretch out for about the same distance as our Moon is from Earth. Jupiter, Neptune and Uranus have rings too but they are smaller than Saturn's.

63

Uranus, Neptune and Pluto

Uranus, Neptune and Pluto are the three outer planets of the Solar System. They are dark frozen worlds because they are a long way from the Sun and get little of its heat and light.

Uranus and Neptune are giant gas planets, like Jupiter and Saturn but smaller. They look greeny blue in colour because of the chemicals they are made of.

Uranus's rings

This is Uranus. It is circled by nine rings. The rings are smaller than Saturn's. They are probably made of rocks and ice.

This is the shadow cast by the rings.

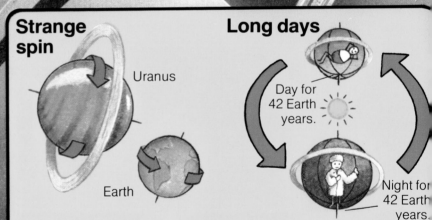

Strange spin

Uranus

Earth

Uranus spins round in a different way to all the other planets. It seems to be lying down, while the others stand up.

Long days

Day for 42 Earth years.

Night for 42 Earth years.

Because of its lying down spin, Uranus has very odd days. On some parts, days and nights are 42 Earth years long.

...o not know very much about these three distant planets. They are so far away they are difficult to see from Earth even with the largest telescopes. The rings around Uranus were discovered in 1977, and Neptune's were found in 1989.

Neptune

As Uranus and Neptune are far from the Sun they have long years. Uranus takes 84 Earth years to orbit the Sun and Neptune takes 165 Earth years.

Uranus and Neptune spin quite fast. Uranus takes about 15½ Earth hours to go round once. Neptune takes about 16 hours.

A spacecraft called Voyager 2 left Earth in 1977. It reached Uranus in 1986 and Neptune in 1989, when it discovered rings around this planet too. It did not land on these planets but flew past them.

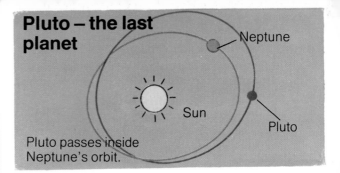

Pluto – the last planet

Pluto passes inside Neptune's orbit.

Tiny Pluto takes 247 Earth years to orbit right round the Sun. For most of this time it is the last planet of the Solar System. But for 20 Earth years of each orbit it passes inside Neptune's orbit, making it the most distant planet. This last happened in 1979.

Discovering Planet X

Until about 1915, Neptune was thought to be the last planet of the Solar System. Then an astronomer, Percival Lowell, worked out that there should be another planet beyond Neptune. He named it Planet X and searched for many years but did not find it.

In 1930 another astronomer, Clyde Tombaugh, was taking photographs of stars. He noticed a stray "star" on the picture which he could not identify. He realised that he had photographed the mysterious Planet X. It was later named Pluto.

Comets

Comets are wandering visitors to the Solar System. About 20 come close to Earth each year but only a few are big and bright enough to be seen without telescopes. Every 10 years or so we might see a big bright comet like the one in this picture.

Comet's tail. Some have forked or double tails.

Comets are not as solid as they look. They are made of gases, ice and specks of dust.

Comets can be very large. One which appeared in 1893 had a tail that stretched out in space from the Sun to Mars.

Comet's head

Meteors

Comets leave bits of dust from their tails behind in space. Earth passes through the dusty places each year and we see a shower of bright shooting stars in the sky. They are called meteors by scientists.

Meteors are specks of comet dust which burn red hot as they fall through Earth's air. Sometimes larger pieces of stray space rock come close to Earth and burn up as they fall through the air.

Big bright comets can be seen from Earth for many weeks or even months.

Some comets can be seen regularly. They reappear after a certain number of years. One famous regular comet is Halley's Comet which returns every 76 years. It will be seen again in 2061.

Comet's path in space

Comets go round the Sun but have differently shaped orbits to the planets. Many come from the outer edges of the Solar System and go round the Sun getting even closer to it than Venus or Mercury do.

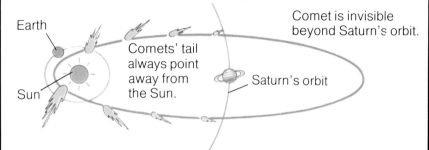

Earth

Comet is invisible beyond Saturn's orbit.

Comets' tail always point away from the Sun.

Sun

Saturn's orbit

Comets do not shine by their own light. They reflect light from the Sun. This means that they are invisible when a long way from the Sun. They start to shine when they get about as close to the Sun as Saturn is.

Meteorites

A crater in Arizona U.S.A. is over 1km (½mi) wide and 175m (575ft) deep.

It was made over 22,000 years ago.

Most meteors are small and burn completely without reaching the ground. A few are big enough to survive the fall and land on Earth.

A landed meteor is called a meteorite. Meteorites often break up as they land. They make a hole in the ground called a crater.

Most meteorites are the size of pebbles but a few are huge. One in Africa weighs 60 tonnes – as much as 12 elephants.

The stars you can see at night are giant balls of hot fiery gases, like the Sun. They look smaller because they are very much further away.

Stars are not all the same. They can be different in size, colour, brightness and temperature. Our Sun is a very common kind of average-size yellow star. Stars can be blue, white, yellow, orange or red.

Stars last for thousands of millions of years but they do not stay the same forever. They change as they get older.

These pictures show the life of a star like our Sun. All stars form in huge clouds of gas and dust.

The dust and gases clump together and begin to heat up. Eventually they get so hot that the clump starts to glow and shine. It has become a star.

Measuring with light

Stars are so far away that scientists have had to invent a new way of measuring the distances between them. They use a unit called a light year.

The nearest star is 4½ light years away. Lots of stars are hundreds of light years away

Pluto is 6 light hours away.

The Sun is 8 light minutes away.

The Moon is 1½ light seconds away.

A light year is the distance that light can travel in one Earth year.

Light is the fastest thing in the Universe. It always travels at the same speed. Light is so fast it can go round the Earth 7½ times a second.

Scientists also use light hours, light minutes and light seconds for things which are closer in space.

The Sun will spend most of its life as a yellow star, shining steadily for about 10,000 million years. Eventually it will swell up and turn from yellow to red and become a Red Giant Star.

Red Giants can be up to a hundred times bigger than the Sun. They are brighter but cooler than the Sun. This type of star is at the end of its life.

Red Giant Star

Stars like the Sun turn into Red Giants and then slowly cool down and shrink. They may puff off their outer layers into space, leaving behind a small, almost dead star, called a White Dwarf Star.

White Dwarf Star

Outer layer of Red Giant puff off into space.

Black Hole

The very biggest stars blow up and leave behind a Black Hole which sucks into itself anything that goes near. Not even light can escape a Black Hole in space.

Supernova

Neutron Star

Neutron Star and gas cloud.

Stars larger than the Sun also swell into Red Giants but they have a more spectacular ending. They blow up with a huge explosion called a Supernova*. Most of them leave behind a cloud of gas and dust with a tiny spinning star, called a Neutron Star, in the centre.

*However, a star does not have to be a Red Giant to become a Supernova. The most spectacular Supernova to occur since 1604 was from a Blue Giant in 1987.

69

Galaxies

Stars are not scattered about the Universe. They are gathered in huge groups, each containing hundreds of millions of stars. These groups are called galaxies. Our Sun is a star in a galaxy called the Milky Way.

Our galaxy measures about 80,000 light years across.

There are more stars in the middle of a galaxy than on the edges.

Our Sun is about here.

There are about 250 thousand million stars in our galaxy.

The Milky Way is shaped rather like a catherine wheel firework. Scientists call it a spiral shaped galaxy.
The picture above shows what the Milky Way would look like from space, seen from above or below. If seen from the side it would look the shape pictured underneath.

Our Sun is about here.

Galactic year

Galaxies do not sit still in space. They spin slowly round and round. One complete spin is called a galactic year. The Milky Way takes 225 million Earth years to spin once.

Other galaxies

The Milky Way is just one of many millions of galaxies that make up the Universe. The galaxies are very far away from each other. The nearest galaxy to the Milky Way is about 160 thousand light years away. Galaxies can be different sizes and shapes. Here are some of the common galactic shapes.

This galaxy is an oval shape.

This galaxy is a spiral shape like the Milky Way. There are lots of spiral shaped galaxies.

Here is another kind of spiral galaxy. It is called a barred spiral.

Some galaxies have uneven shapes. This one is almost round.

The Big Bang

Most scientists believe that the Universe began with a huge explosion about 15,000 million years ago. They call this the Big Bang. There are no words to describe what things were like before the Big Bang.

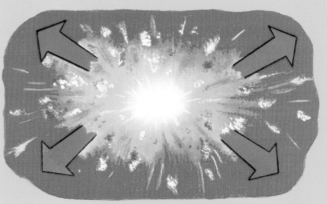

When the Big Bang explosion happened, everything which is in the Universe went flying out in all directions. Scientists say the galaxies formed from the lumps which were flung out by the Big Bang.

The galaxies are still flying away from each other today. No one knows if this will go on forever or if they will stop eventually.

Space words

Here are some of the special space words which have been used in this book.

Years

A planet's year is the length of time it takes to go once round the Sun. Each planet has a different length year.

Days

All of the planets spin round and round. The time a planet takes to spin once is its day. The spinning moves different parts of the surface to face the Sun, giving the planet day-time and night-time.

Moons

A moon is a ball of rock which orbits round a planet. Scientists think that the rings which go round some planets may be made from a moon which broke up or did not form properly.

Asteroids

An asteroid is a piece of rock floating in space. There is a band of thousands of asteroids between the planets Mars and Jupiter.

Meteors

A meteor is a piece of space rock which gets very close to Earth (or another planet) and falls through the air. It burns up as it falls.

Meteorites

Meteors which land on a moon or planet are called meteorites. Most are made of stone but a few are made of iron or stone and iron.

Craters

A crater is the hole made by a meteorite. All of the rocky planets and moons have some craters on their surfaces.

Comets

Comets go round the Sun in long oval orbits. They have been called dirty snowballs in space because they are made of ice and dust.

Sunspots

Sunspots are dark patches on the Sun. They are areas of gas which are cooler than the surface. This makes them seem dark compared to the hotter surface.

Light years

A light year is the unit used for measuring long distances in space. It is the distance that light travels in one Earth year which is 9½ million million km (6 million million mi).

Supernova

A Supernova is an exploding star. Since the year 1006, four exploding stars have been seen in our Galaxy. Some are so bright we can even see them in other galaxies.

Galaxies

A galaxy is a collection of millions and millions of stars. Galaxies can be different shapes and sizes. There are millions of them in the Universe.

Milky Way

We are part of a galaxy which is called the Milky Way, or sometimes just The Galaxy.

Universe

The Universe is everything that exists, all the millions of galaxies, stars, planets and moons that there are.

Index

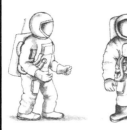

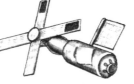

First published in 1982 by
Usborne Publishing Ltd,
Usborne House,
83-85 Saffron Hill,
London, EC1N 8RT.

© 1993, 1989, 1982 Usborne
Publishing Ltd. All rights
reserved. No part of this
publication may be reproduced,
stored in a retrieval system or

transmitted in any form, or by
any means, electronic,
mechanical, photocopying or
otherwise without the prior
permission of the publisher.

The name Usborne and the
device 🐝 are Trade Marks of
Usborne Publishing Ltd.

Printed in Belgium